FANGS

OF EVIL

BULLSEYE CHILLERS™

FANGS
OF EVIL

By Ellen Steiber

BULLSEYE CHILLERS™

RANDOM HOUSE 🏠 NEW YORK

To my friends in Chagford,
especially Alan Lee, who showed me the moorlands,
Mike Scholey, who answered all my questions,
and Terri Windling, who told me I had to see Dartmoor
and then made it possible

A BULLSEYE BOOK PUBLISHED BY RANDOM HOUSE, INC.

Library of Congress Cataloging-in-Publication Data:
Steiber, Ellen
Fangs of evil / by Ellen Steiber.
p. cm. — (Bullseye chillers) Based on: The boy who drew cats /
rendered into English by Lafcadio Hearn.
SUMMARY: In nineteenth-century Devon, England, farms and families
are being ravaged by an unknown, seemingly inhuman killer, and
twelve-year-old Elizabeth, considered strange because she spends all her
time drawing cats, is suspected by the superstitious townspeople.
ISBN 0-679-85466-5
[1. Dartmoor (England)—Fiction. 2. Cats—Fiction.
3. Horror stories.] I. Hearn, Lafcadio, 1850-1904. Boy who drew cats.
II. Title. III. Series.
PZ7.S81766Fan 1994 [Fic]—dc20 93-44043

Manufactured in the United States of America 10 9 8 7 6 5 4 3

CONTENTS

Chapter 1
The Beginning

When I was twelve years old, I was sent away from my father's house. Strange things were happening on the moor. Most of our neighbors thought I had something to do with them. You see, I was an odd child. I was no good at mending shirts. I didn't want to clean the house. I forgot to milk the cows. When I was told to weed the garden, I wandered into the wood. I wasn't even very good at schoolwork.

My father said I'd never marry. I thought he was right. I was too thin to be pretty. I was too willful to charm a man. And even my little sister was a far better cook.

I loved my family and tried to be a good daughter. But the truth is, there was only one thing I wanted to do. I wanted to draw cats. I drew the cats who lived in our barn. I drew the baker's kittens and the doctor's lazy tom. I drew cats even when there were no cats in sight. I couldn't help it.

We lived on a small sheep farm in Devon. My mother died just after my youngest brother was born. That left my father to raise the five of us on his own.

My sister and brothers did just what they should. My two older brothers helped my father herd the sheep. They also gathered and dried the peat we burned in our hearth. Jenny, my younger sister, had a talent for all I lacked. She cooked and sewed and cleaned. James, the youngest, cared for the chickens. But there was very little that I did that came out right.

When things got bad in Devon, people looked for something or someone to blame. And just because I was different, the people in the village said I was the root of all the problems. Even my own father could not prove them wrong. I do not blame my father for sending me away. We were all very scared.

We lived on Dartmoor, you see. The moor is like no other place. It is a wide open land with green hills as far as the eye can see. It is also a haunted land. Some people say Dartmoor has so many ghosts and spirits that it's a wonder there's any room for the living.

My brother Will claims that he was chased once by giant hounds with eyes of fire. Mrs. Potter saw the fairy folk dancing in Wistman's Wood. Old Man Crane has seen ghost monks carrying a coffin. And Edwina still sees mysterious lights in the fog

I don't know if any of those stories are true. But the story I am about to tell is true. It happened in 1876, when I was twelve years old. That is when things in Braunton began to disappear. And to die.

Chapter 2

The First Death

Edwina put her hands on her hips. "Can't you walk faster, Elizabeth?" she asked me. "We'll never get to town."

Edwina, who was two years older than I, lived on the farm next to ours. We were walking in the narrow lane that led to the village of Braunton. Edwina wanted to buy cloth for a dress. I was to buy buttons for my brother's shirt.

It was early summer. The days were still cool. Lambs and ponies wandered the fields. The old stone wall that edged the lane was covered with dark green ivy and pink foxglove. The road beneath our feet was thick, wet mud.

"Elizabeth," Edwina said. "Why are you stopping?"

I pointed over the wall. "Something is wrong at Dr. Shaw's house," I said.

Dr. Shaw was standing outside his house. His four sons were outside too, lined up in front of the barn.

"Where is it?" the doctor shouted. "A shed full of grain doesn't just empty itself!"

"Come on!" Edwina tugged on my sleeve. "It's not polite to listen."

Sometimes Edwina had no curiosity at all.

So we kept walking. But I wondered about Dr. Shaw. His youngest son, Jeremy, was my age. We were friends. Dr.

Shaw was very kind to his patients. But he was very strict with his sons. I hoped Jeremy wasn't in trouble.

Edwina and I started down the hill that led into Braunton. I loved going to the village. It smelled of fresh-baked bread and peat smoke. Cottages lined the narrow cobblestone lanes. The cottages were white. They had thatched roofs and window boxes filled with flowers.

Farmers brought their vegetables and cheeses to the market in the village square. Neighbors gathered in front of the shops to talk.

Edwina and I went into Mrs. Crosby's shop. I bought the buttons for my brother's shirt and some blue thread for Jenny. Then I had to wait while Edwina decided which fabric to buy. It was so silly. Edwina always chose brown. But she always took half a day to make up her mind. While Edwina was deciding, I wandered back outside.

The brown tabby who lived in the pub was sitting in the sunshine, washing her face. I took out the stick of charcoal I kept in my pocket. I sat down on a doorstep and watched the cat. Then I drew her on the paper bag that held the buttons and the thread. The cat's stripes faded a bit on her tail. I smudged the charcoal, trying to get that right.

"Stop it, girl!" said a brisk voice behind me. The Widow Stevens stood over me, frowning. As always, she was dressed in black. Even her earrings were jet. Shiny bits of black.

She reached down and grabbed the bag from my hands. "More useless drawings!" she said. "You can't even bake a proper pie!"

The cat fled. I stood up. "Could I please have my bag back?" I asked. "It has buttons for Will's shirt."

Widow Stevens glared at the bag. Then she gave it back to me. "Someone ought to talk to your father," she said. "A man can't be expected to raise a daughter properly."

"Jenny's doing fine," I pointed out.

She shook a finger in my face. "Don't talk to me like that!" she scolded. "I wish I had the schooling of you. Then you'd learn how to be a young lady!"

"Yes, Mrs. Stevens." I knew better than to argue.

"Do you know what happens to lazy girls?" she demanded. "The ghosts of the moor come after them. I know because they took my poor husband. Late at night when everyone else is asleep—"

At that moment Edwina came out of Mrs. Crosby's shop. Edwina knew exactly what was happening.

"Good morning, Mrs. Stevens," she said. "It's a beautiful morning, isn't it?" Edwina was wonderful at saying all the polite things that adults like.

Widow Stevens thought Edwina was perfect. She told her what a lovely young lady she was. Then she went off on her errands.

"Widow Stevens doesn't think I'm being raised right," I told Edwina.

"Mrs. Stevens is an old busybody!" Edwina said. "Let's have a quick look around before we start for home. Don't let her worry you."

But the widow did worry me. I wondered if the ghosts of the moor would come after me. I thought about what she said all the way along the twisting lane. I thought about her until we saw Jeremy Shaw. He was riding his mare across the moor. The wind blew his hair and the horse's mane straight back. They were both the same deep brown.

"Jeremy!" I waved to him and he waved back.

"I need to talk to Jeremy," I told Edwina. "Tell my father I'll be home in a bit."

"Your dad won't like that," Edwina said. "He said you were to come straight home."

I knew she was right, but I was curious. I wanted to know about the grain.

"Don't worry," I said. "I'll be home soon."

I ran to catch up with Jeremy. He stopped the horse.

"What are you doing?" I asked.

"Looking for one of Mum's sheep," he replied. "The little brown one's gone missing. She didn't come back with the rest of the flock."

"What happened at your house today?" I asked. "Edwina and I heard your father shouting."

Jeremy frowned. "They probably heard him all the way in Braunton. Someone got into our shed. They stole all the grain we stored for winter."

"Maybe it was an animal," I said.

Jeremy shook his head. "It couldn't be. The floor was swept clean. Not a single grain was left. My father thought one of us had played a joke."

"Did you?" I asked. Jeremy and his brothers were known for their pranks.

Jeremy shook his head. "None of us knows who did it."

In the distance something howled. I shivered. "Maybe that's one of the ghost hounds."

"Don't you start that, too," Jeremy said. "There are no such things as ghosts or spirits. That was probably a dog howling. I keep telling you, everything has a scientific explanation."

"And you sound just like your father," I told him.

Jeremy rolled his eyes. "I've got a sheep to find. I'll see you later, Elizabeth."

I started off toward our farm. But I didn't get far. I walked to the top of a rise and started screaming. I couldn't help myself. I'd found Mrs. Shaw's lost ewe. The poor thing's throat was cut. Part of her side was torn out. And her brown woolly coat was covered with blood.

Chapter 3

Mysterious Happenings

Jeremy took the sheep back to his home. He showed it to his father. Dr. Shaw said it must have been killed by a fox. Or maybe someone's dog. Jeremy buried the sheep. No one ever found out who stole the grain.

Old Man Crane was the next to report strange happenings. He lived in a tiny stone cottage just outside the village. Mr. Crane drove his cart everywhere, even though his eyes were bad. He said his horse, Robert, saw for both of them.

One morning, not long after the Shaws lost their sheep, Old Man Crane drove his cart up to our house.

"I've been robbed!" he cried.

Rain was pouring down. But we all ran out to see what the matter was.

"They emptied my cupboard!" he said. "I went to market yesterday. I filled my cupboard full of food. This morning it's empty!"

"Now, Henry," said my father. "Maybe you're not looking in the right places."

Then my father sent me and my older brother Gabe back to Old Man Crane's house. He told us to find the lost food.

Gabe and I searched every inch of that house. It didn't take very long. The cottage was tiny. The cupboard wasn't even as wide as I was. There wasn't a scrap of food to be found.

Gabe scratched his head. "Do you think Old Man Crane's mind is going?" he asked. "Maybe he never went to market yesterday."

So Gabe and I went into the village. Three different people had seen Old Man Crane buy his food and take it home.

"He was telling the truth," I said. "Someone broke into his house and cleaned out his cupboard."

"Someone hungry," Gabe said.

We went home and told my father what we'd found. That night Old Man Crane stayed to dinner.

Early the next morning I was in the barn. I was supposed to be milking the cow. But first, of course, I wanted to draw the gray barn cat. He'd gotten into the rafters. He was sitting on a wooden beam, with one paw dangling down.

I was sketching him on the wall of the barn when Jenny came running in. "Elizabeth, where are you?" she cried.

"Here," I said, standing up. "What's wrong?"

"Didn't you see the field?" she asked me. Her eyes were filled with tears.

I followed my sister outside to the field where our sheep grazed. My father and brothers stood there silently. The day before, bright green grass had covered the field. Now I stared at bare earth.

"I-I don't understand," I said.

"The grass is gone!" Jenny said. "It was taken during the night."

"Who could take a field full of grass?" my father asked.

Or a shed full of grain? I thought.

"What are you going to do?" I asked my father. I knew he would have to find another place to graze our animals.

"I don't know, lass," he told me. He gave me a sharp look. "Have you milked the cow yet?"

"No, Dad," I replied.

"Then do it quickly," he said. A smile flickered around his mouth as he added, "Before someone steals the cow."

I don't think any of us imagined that within the month the cow would be gone too. And the pig and the chickens. We found them all with their throats cut and their limbs gone.

We weren't the only ones to suffer.

Every farm on our part of the moor was hit. Farm animals were killed. Grain, corn, meal, flour, vegetables—everything disappeared. Men kept watch with their dogs. The village constable sent two men to patrol the farms.

No one ever found a thief. Or even the traces of one. And yet the raids went on.

One rainy night our neighbors gathered at our house. The wind blew hard outside. My father sat at the head of the long table in the kitchen. "Our farms are being destroyed," he said.

"The animals are starving. There will be no wool or milk to sell," he went on. "I don't know what we'll do."

Mrs. Potter's voice shook as she spoke. "We're all going to starve," she said. "It doesn't even pay to plant again. I put in new tomato plants last week. They were gone this morning."

"You think that's bad?" Edwina's father asked. "I closed my sheep in the barn last night. I locked the door with a heavy padlock. This morning the padlock lay on the ground. The sheep were all dead. Torn to pieces."

"There has to be an explanation," said Dr. Shaw. "This can't be the work of an animal. No animal is strong enough to break into locked sheds. No animal can clear a field. Our thief has to be a man."

"Why would a man kill all those animals?" Edwina's father shuddered. "It looked as if he ate parts of them."

Widow Stevens stood up. She pounded her cane on the floor. "Listen to me, all of you!" she said. "This thief is no human. And no animal. This is the work of Evil!"

"Oh, Maddy," Dr. Shaw said. "What *are* you talking about?"

Jeremy, who was sitting next to his father, looked at me and grinned. He didn't like the widow, either.

"What I'm talking about has no scientific explanation," Mrs. Stevens said.

"Then it doesn't exist," Dr. Shaw said briskly.

"Evil exists!" Widow Stevens said loudly. "It's here in this room with us."

The wind rose as she spoke. The wooden shutter above the sink suddenly blew open. The candles in the center of the table went out.

"Elizabeth, go find the flint," my father said calmly.

The gas lamp on the wall was still

lit. So it wasn't hard to find the stone flint. I gave it to my father. He relit the candles.

"Don't you see?" the widow said. "That's proof!"

"Of what?" my brother Will asked. "A windstorm?"

"That Evil really exists," the widow answered. "Evil lives in those too idle to keep it out." My mouth dropped open as the widow pointed a bony finger at me. "Your own daughter Elizabeth is the cause of all this trouble!"

"What?" my father said.

"That's a foolish idea!" Dr. Shaw said. "You can't blame a child for any of this."

"What does she do all day?" the widow demanded. "She draws cats! Do you call that normal for a girl her age? She can't even do the work her younger sister does. Mark my words. Elizabeth Colwin is the cause of all your troubles. Send her away and your troubles will end."

I was shaking, too shocked to speak. But no one else was. Arguments broke out all over the room. My father and Dr. Shaw said the widow just wanted to blame someone. My brother Will said she was daft.

"Mind your tongue, Will," my father said sharply.

"The girl belongs to the Darkness," the widow insisted.

A few of our neighbors thought she was right. Mrs. Potter said the widow understood the secrets of the moor better than most. Everyone had to agree with that.

Finally, the widow stood up again. She nodded at our neighbors. "We must act quickly," she said. "The girl who draws cats is the source of the Evil. No farm in Devon will be safe until she's sent away."

Chapter 4

River Dart Takes a Heart

That night the wind raged until nearly dawn. I woke just before the first light broke. The storm was over. I think the quiet woke me. Jenny was awake, too. She sat up in bed, peering through the window. Outside, the sky was still dark.

"Jenny?" I said.

She turned. Her blond hair lay loose about her shoulders. "What is it?"

"Do you believe what Widow Stevens said last night? That I'm the cause of all the trouble?"

Jenny laughed. "Of course not! No one with any sense believes her."

"Then why did she say it?" I asked.

Jenny sighed. "Widow Stevens is just a superstitious woman."

"What do you think is eating things?" I asked.

Jenny gazed out the window again. "I don't know," she answered. "And I don't think anyone else knows either."

We were both silent for a while. Then Jenny asked, "Elizabeth, why *do* you draw all those cats?"

"I don't know," I said honestly. "It's just something I do."

"Is it fun?" she asked.

"I suppose," I answered. "I don't really think about it. When I draw cats, it's—it's because I want to understand."

"Understand *what?*" Jenny asked.

I knew I was not being clear. Jenny was a very bright ten-year-old.

"Sorry," I said. "I've never explained this before, even to myself." I thought awhile. "It's like this," I said. "When I see a cat, just seeing it is not enough. Cats are so beautiful that I want to really know them. I want to know what it feels like to be a cat sleeping in the sun. Or a cat hunting a bird. But they can't talk. So I can't know them the way you know a person. That's why I draw them."

Jenny looked at me as if I'd lost my mind. "I don't think you're evil," she said. "But you *are* a little odd."

Through the window we could see the sunrise. Somewhere in the distance a rooster crowed.

"Come on," Jenny said. "It's time to get up."

Whatever was raiding the farms attacked only at night. The dead animals and razed fields were always found in the morning. Soon everyone in Dartmoor dreaded waking up. Each morning, people opened their eyes and thought, "What happened last night? What was destroyed? What awful thing will I find?"

The only good thing was that no one talked any more about sending me away. Everyone seemed to forget what Widow Stevens had said. They said a goblin was to blame.

Our family lost our fields and most of our farm animals. The barn cats weren't touched. I thought they must have been very good at hiding. Sometimes I would look at them in the morning and wonder.

"What was out there last night?" I asked the gray tom. "What was walking the moor?"

He didn't answer, of course. He purred and washed his toes. But I knew he knew. Cats see everything that happens at night.

"Dart, Dart, River Dart. Every year you take a heart," Laura sang out. Laura was Edwina's younger sister.

"Ah, that's just an old story," Jeremy said.

Jeremy, Laura, Edwina, and I sat on the riverbank. It was a lazy Sunday afternoon. We'd all gone to church that morning. We'd all prayed for the evil on the moor to end.

"It's a true story!" Laura insisted. "Listen to the river. You can hear it calling for a heart. Last year Sally Hoskins drowned. Now it wants someone else."

Jeremy rolled his eyes. "All I hear is water running over rocks," he said.

"No," Laura said. "Listen carefully. Listen to what the river is saying. Someone is going to die today."

"Laura, stop it!" Edwina snapped. "Aren't things scary enough already?"

Jeremy stood up. He picked up a pebble and threw it into the water. "There," he said. "I gave the river a pebble. Now it won't bother anyone."

Laura put her hands on her hips. "Laugh if you want!" she said. "But I know—"

She stopped talking. Mrs. Potter was coming toward us. Her children were with her. Mary was ten. Gordon was three. Gordon was a funny little boy. He always toddling off somewhere. They said he even walked in his sleep. Now his mother held his hand firmly. It was hard for him to walk as fast as the others.

"Good afternoon!" Mrs. Potter called out.

"Afternoon," we all replied.

"Mrs. Potter," Laura said. "Do you know the poem about the river?"

"Don't speak of it!" Mrs. Potter said sharply.

"It's true, then," Laura said. "Isn't it? Someone else is going to drown."

"They don't always drown," Mary said. "Sometimes they die at home."

"Hush, Mary!" her mother said.

"Ush!" Gordon repeated. His mother smiled and let go of his hand.

"What do you think, Elizabeth?" Laura asked.

I didn't know. I wanted to believe that Jeremy was right. That the old rhyme didn't mean anything. But someone did drown every year.

"I'm not sure," I said. "I don't know what would explain it. But then, so many things on the moor just can't be explained."

Mrs. Potter gave me an odd look. "Like you drawing all those cats?"

Gordon toddled toward the river. "Gordon!" his mother shrieked. She snatched him back to her side.

Jeremy looked bored. He had tied his mare to the branch of an oak tree. Now he untied her. "I'm going home," he said. He made a face at Laura. "Before the river gets me."

"We're on our way, too," Mrs. Potter

said. She gave me another odd look. Then she and her children walked off.

That left Edwina and Laura and me. The river flowed clear and calm before us. We could see straight to the bottom. Minnows swam between moss-covered rocks.

"It's hard to believe anyone drowns," Edwina said. "The water isn't very deep."

"It's because of the river god," Laura said seriously. "He needs a new heart every year. So every year he calls to his victim."

This time Edwina stood up. "River gods!" she said. "Next you'll be asking me to believe in talking turnips!"

Edwina stalked off. Laura trailed after her.

I stayed by the river, watching the dragonflies play on the water. Before I knew it, I'd picked up a sharp stone. I began to trace lines in the dirt bank. The curved line of a cat's back. Two sharp points for its ears . . . For a while I forgot about river gods and goblins. For a while I was happy.

The next afternoon I was digging in the garden. The air was cool and misty. My father had told me to plant potatoes.

I hated planting potatoes. That morning I'd argued with my father.

"It's too late to plant," I told him. "The potatoes will only be half grown before the frost sets in."

"Then we'll eat small potatoes," he said. "It's better than starving. Do as I tell you, lass. Or else there'll be no food this winter."

I had hoed the ditches for the water.

I had placed the sprouted chunks of potato in the furrows. Now I covered them carefully.

I looked up as I heard hoofbeats pounding. Jeremy was galloping toward me. Something had to be wrong. His mare was an old horse. He never made her run that fast.

"Elizabeth!" he shouted.

"What is it?" I asked. I stood up and wiped the dirt from my hands.

He brought the horse to a stop. Both boy and horse were breathing hard.

"The Widow Stevens," he said. "She's coming this way. She has others with her. You have to leave before she gets here!"

"What's this all about?" my father asked. He had come from the barn when he saw Jeremy ride up.

"Mrs. Potter. The Widow Stevens," Jeremy panted.

"Talk sense, boy!" my father snapped.

"It's little Gordon Potter," Jeremy explained. "Last night he left his bed. Went walking in his sleep. They found him by the River Dart this morning. His throat was ripped open. And a chunk had been taken out of his chest. Like—like what's happened to the farm animals."

I remembered Laura saying the River Dart would take a heart. I started to shake. "And poor little Gordon is dead?" I asked.

Jeremy nodded. "And you have to leave, Elizabeth. You have to go some-place far away."

"Why?" I asked. "What have I got to do with Gordon Potter's death?"

"Mrs. Potter says you're to blame," Jeremy answered. "She sent for the Widow Stevens. They say the cats you draw are some sort of evil magic."

"They're not!" I cried. "They're just drawings!"

"Elizabeth, hush!" my father said.

"They said your cats are what killed Gordon," Jeremy went on. "Widow Stevens heard howling last night. She thinks the cats called Gordon to the riverbank."

"Nonsense!" I said. "I've never heard anything so stupid."

"Stupid or not, they've gone to Braunton for the constable," Jeremy said. "They want you arrested for murder!"

Chapter 5

The Widow Is Believed

I tried to make sense of what Jeremy had told me. How could anyone believe that my drawings were evil magic? How could anyone believe that a few lines on paper could kill a small boy?

I turned to my father. "You won't let the constable arrest me, will you?"

My father didn't answer me.

"When did Mrs. Potter and the widow go into Braunton?" he asked Jeremy.

"Just a bit after two," Jeremy said.

He sounded sick. "It was so sad. Mrs. Potter wouldn't believe Gordon was dead. She called for my father. I went with him. He examined Gordon and said there was nothing he could do. That's when Mrs. Potter went for Widow Stevens. I followed her."

My father pulled his watch from his pocket. "It's nearly four," he said. "They could be here soon."

"Well, just tell them they're daft!" I said.

"That may not do any good," my father said sadly.

I began to feel the way I feel at the beginning of a nightmare. Even before anything bad happens, there's a moment when the terror starts. It feels as if the whole world has suddenly gone dark.

"What about your father?" I asked

Jeremy. "He can't think I killed Gordon."

"No," Jeremy agreed. "My dad said some sort of animal did it. Same one that's been killing the livestock."

"What did Mrs. Potter say to that?" I asked.

Jeremy ran a hand through his hair. "She said that it was your drawings that called up the animal."

I tried not to sound as afraid as I felt. "Surely the constable won't believe such nonsense."

My father gave me a long, cold look. "No one's ever found out what's killed all the animals," he said. "Everyone's looking for a cause. Even the constable."

"Look, we'll get your father," I told Jeremy. "He'll tell the constable I had nothing to do with this."

"My dad won't be back for a while," Jeremy said. "Mrs. Finley's having a baby."

Mrs. Finley lived clear across the moor. It was a day's ride either way.

I started to shake all over again. Even my knees trembled.

"How can this be happening?" I asked. "It's like a bad dream. It's—"

"Elizabeth, stop muttering! Go pack a bag," my father ordered.

"Why?" I asked. "You know my drawings aren't magic or evil. It's a lie."

My father started to shout. "I'm telling you to get out of here before Widow Stevens arrives! And for once you'll obey me without an argument!"

I should have done as he asked. But I couldn't believe what I was hearing. Worse, I couldn't believe what I was seeing. There was a strange look in my father's eyes.

"You—you're afraid of me!" I said. "You actually believe them! You think my drawings are evil. You think I killed Gordon Potter!"

I felt my father's hand crack hard against my cheek. "Get out!" he said. "For heaven's sake, lass. Get out while you still can!"

Chapter 6

Escape!

I went upstairs to the room I shared with Jenny. Dazed, I packed a clean dress, a nightgown, underwear, and a comb. I also took a small box of drawing charcoal. I'd bought it last spring when Aunt Sarah sent me a shilling for my birthday.

I put everything in a cloth sack. I didn't know what else to take. I didn't know where I was going. All I knew was that my father had sent me out of the house. And I was going to have to run for my life.

Jenny saw me as I came back down the stairs. "Elizabeth," she said. "Where are you going? And what's the sack for?"

I couldn't tell her what had happened. I was ashamed. And I was afraid I'd cry.

"I'll tell you when I get back," I said. "Dad said I had to hurry." I hugged her and ran outside.

Jeremy and his mare stood by the garden. My father was gone.

"Where's my father?" I asked.

"He—he had to go," Jeremy said quickly. "One of the fences was falling down and—"

"You're lying," I said.

Jeremy nodded. "He's very upset. He says it's best if he doesn't know where you're going."

"You mean my own father might give me away?" I could not quite believe this was really happening to me.

"He said to tell you to be careful," Jeremy went on. "And to behave yourself."

I gazed out across the lonely moor. I felt the way I did when I was four years old and got lost in a fog. I felt as if I might wander forever. And no one would ever find me. I felt as if I might never see my way back home.

"Where am I going to go?" I asked bleakly.

Jeremy sighed and held out a hand to me. "Get on," he said. "We'll think of something."

Jeremy didn't know where to go either. He just set off across the moor, riding away from Braunton. I sat in front, holding my sack tightly.

Behind me, Jeremy held the reins.

Gretchen, his mare, took her time. She was tired from the gallop to my house. Now she walked so slowly that I was afraid she'd fall asleep.

"Is this horse all right?" I asked Jeremy.

"She's fine," he said. "But she's twenty-six years old." He didn't need to say that twenty-six was old for a horse.

"Can't you make her go faster?" I asked.

"No, I can't," he told me.

"Then let me off," I said. "I want to walk."

"Elizabeth," Jeremy said. "Don't panic!"

"I can't help it," I told him. "Mrs. Potter wants me arrested for murder. And my own father seems to think she's right. They're hunting me. And I don't know where to go and—" Suddenly I was crying. I stuffed my fist in my mouth but that didn't help.

Jeremy stopped the horse. His arms went around me. He pulled me against him. For a while we sat there like that, him holding me, me sobbing.

"It's all right," he said. "You'll see. It will all come out right."

People always say that when you're crying. I've never believed any of them. Still, it felt good to hear Jeremy say it. I didn't want to sit there in the middle of the moor, bawling.

I dried my eyes. "I'm fine now," I said.

"And I'm the Queen of England," he teased.

I sniffed and wiped my nose with a handkerchief. "Let's go."

"Where to, my lady?" Jeremy's voice

was still teasing. But his question was serious. Where to indeed?

I pointed west across the moor. "Let's just get as far away from Braunton as we can."

Jeremy frowned. "I've got to go home. My mum doesn't know I came after you. She'll have kittens if I don't show up tonight."

"I'll hide somewhere," I said bravely. "Let's ride to one of the tors."

On the moor, tors are what you call the big, craggy boulders on the tops of many hills. If a tor is big enough, there are dozens of hiding places in it. I once spent hours searching for my little brother when he hid at Great Hound Tor.

We rode west, crossing hill after hill. The sheep and wild ponies kept us company. The ponies were interested in Gretchen. Gretchen was interested in going home. She kept fighting Jeremy. Jeremy pushed her on.

"Come on, girl," he said. "I promise you warm mash tonight."

Gretchen came to a dead stop as we reached one of the old stone circles. No one really knows who built the stone circles. Or why. But they've been there forever. You find them scattered across the moor. Strange circles made from giant stones spaced wide apart.

Our teacher in school said the standing stones go back to the Bronze Age. All sorts of stories are told about them. Some folks say they're gateways to other times. Others say you can use a circle to predict the solstice—the two days each year when the sun is farthest from the equator. The stone circles are thought to be full of old magic, like just about everything on the moor.

Gretchen certainly seemed to think so. This circle was a huge one. We wanted to ride through it because it would take much longer to go around it. The mare refused. Jeremy coaxed her. Then he threatened her. He dug his heels into her sides. Finally, the two of us got off. He tried to pull her by the bridle.

He might as well have tried to move one of the stones. Gretchen wasn't having any of it. Her eyes were wide with terror. Her mouth foamed. She reared up on her hind legs, whinnying.

"Let her be, Jeremy!" I said. "The circle scares her."

Jeremy glared at me. "The last thing

I need is a superstitious horse," he said. "It's bad enough that people are so foolish."

"Maybe she's not so foolish," I said. "Maybe she sees or hears something that we can't. Animals have sharper senses than humans."

The sun had begun to set by then. Dusk was creeping across the moor. The standing stones cast long shadows against the grass. There *was* something eerie about the circle. I didn't want to enter it any more than Gretchen did.

"Let's go around," I said.

"It'll be midnight before I'm home," Jeremy muttered. But he led the mare around the circle.

That saved my life. As we walked around we came to a bit of higher ground that looked toward Braunton. A line of people snaked over the hills.

Some of them were carrying torches. Bloodhounds ran ahead of them.

"Jeremy, look!" I said. I suddenly felt sick to my stomach.

Jeremy squinted into the distance. "I can't make out who they are," he said. "They're too far away."

"They're looking for me," I said. I couldn't really see them either. But I knew exactly who they were. "It's the widow and Mrs. Potter and the constable. And a crowd is following them."

Jeremy bit his lip. Then he nodded.

"Get back on the horse," he said. "I believe you're right."

Chapter 7

Across the Moor

Jeremy said that our best hope was that the dogs would search for my scent. And not Gretchen's. He pushed the old mare faster. Now that we were past the stone circle, she began to trot. We crossed hill after hill.

I didn't know how far we'd gone. Or where we were. We were well beyond our own part of the moor. The tors here were unfamiliar. Each was different from the one before. Yet we'd ridden so long, I couldn't tell them apart. My sense of direction was gone. I was lost.

From time to time, we'd climb to the peak of a tor to look back. Always the line of villagers was in sight. Their torches blazed through the darkness.

"They're not giving up," I said.

"I'm hungry," Jeremy said. "What sort of food did you bring?"

"I didn't bring any," I replied.

"Well, then, how about some water?"

"None of that either," I admitted.

"Oh, that's brilliant!" he shouted. "You left home and didn't bother to bring food. What did you think you were going to eat? Grass? Or rocks, maybe? We could have a lovely earthworm stew!"

"Stop shouting!" I said crossly. "I didn't think about food. I was too upset."

Jeremy nudged Gretchen into a walk. "I'm sorry," he said quietly. "Look, there's a large tor up ahead. Let's find a hiding place for you. Then I'll go home before Mum sends out a search party to look for *me*."

I swallowed hard. No matter what, I wasn't going to cry again. I tried to sound brave. "That's a good plan," I said. "I'll be fine on my own."

"Without food and water? I'm sure you'll be grand," he agreed sarcastically.

I wanted to ask him to stay. I didn't want to be left alone on the moor. Especially with the dogs after me. But Jeremy had done enough. I couldn't ask him for more.

"Elizabeth, I'm not going to just dump you," Jeremy said. "I'll come back in the morning. I'll bring some food."

"And then what?"

"I don't know," Jeremy answered. "I just don't know."

A short while later Gretchen climbed a hill thick with bracken. At the top were huge white boulders. It was one of the larger tors. A mist had fallen with the night. We couldn't tell where the boulders stopped. But the granite rocks seemed almost as large as those on Great Hound Tor. A legend says the rocks there were once giant hounds who were turned to stone. I looked up at the huge boulder that towered above me. Was it once something else? I wondered. Something changed by magic?

Jeremy let Gretchen graze. He and I walked around the boulders. At last we settled on a narrow cave on the far side of the tor. The cave was hard to reach and even harder to squeeze into. I had to climb a steep ledge to reach it. But Will had taught me to climb. And I'd always liked scrambling into tight spots that no one else could manage. At least there was one useful thing about being so skinny.

"This should keep me out of the wind," I said.

"Aye," Jeremy agreed. "Don't light a fire, though. You don't want to draw attention."

"No chance of that," I said. "I don't have a flint."

Jeremy rolled his eyes. "I'll bring you a flint tomorrow. Did you at least pack a sweater?"

I shook my head. Jeremy took off his sweater and handed it to me.

"Don't freeze to death or go off wandering," he ordered. "I'll be back as soon as I can."

"Right," I said. I was too tired to tell him he was being bossy. And, in fact, for once I really didn't mind.

Jeremy got back on his horse. "Good night, Elizabeth," he said softly.

"Good night," I said. "And Jeremy—"

"What?"

"Thank you."

Jeremy rode out of sight almost at once. The sound of Gretchen's hooves reached me long after I could see her. Fog cloaked the moor like a thick, damp blanket. It swallowed up horse and rider. It swallowed the sheep who bleated nearby. I hoped Jeremy would be able to find his way home. And I prayed that the fog would make the constable turn back.

I couldn't stop thinking about the search party. What would they do when they found me? Take me to jail, certainly. And then I'd be tried. I'd probably be hanged. Hanged for killing a child by drawing cats! I still couldn't believe any of it.

I was tired. But I was too frightened to sleep. In spite of the darkness, I climbed to the top of the tor. I looked out across the moor. In every direction the view was the same. Mist and more mist. Behind the cloud cover was a full moon. Though it was hidden, its light filtered through the fog. All around me the night sky glowed a dull silver-white.

And then I saw something cut through the fog. Burning yellow light—

the torches. And I heard the sound of
hounds barking frantically.

Chapter 8

In Hiding

I tried to scramble down from the top of the tor. But I couldn't move. Fear froze every muscle in my body. The search party hadn't turned back. They hadn't gotten lost in the fog. I don't think it had even slowed them down. What was I going to do?

I forced myself to breathe deeply. My breath seemed to unlock my limbs. Slowly, quietly, I made my way to the cave. Maybe they would find me here. But the cave was hard to reach and harder to get into. It felt safer than fleeing across the moor with dogs at my heels.

Then I did something that made no sense. It was pure habit. I reached into my pocket and took out my piece of charcoal. The inside of the cave was black. But I didn't need to see. At the very base of the rock I began to draw by feel. The lines were all as familiar as my own hands. The arch of a cat's back. The curve of its tail. The straight fine lines of the whiskers...

Can this really be dark magic? I wondered. Could drawings of cats harm a small boy? Could they call up evil powers? If any of those things were true...I couldn't bear to think of it.

I'd been terrified ever since I learned of Gordon's death. I was cold and tired and hungry. The constable wanted to arrest me for murder. I could hear the voices of the search party. They were getting even closer. But now my fear was gone. I felt safe. Drawing made me feel as if I'd found home.

I finished the drawing of the cat. It was just a small one. Then I put on Jeremy's sweater. And I curled up on the cold cave floor and slept.

When I awoke it was still night. Perhaps only an hour or so had passed. I could hear the sounds of the search party. They were very close now. I could hear them tramping through the bracken just beneath the tor.

The constable's voice carried clearly. "We've been all over this part of the moor. I tell you, there's nothing here!"

"But the dogs!" That was the postmaster's voice. "The dogs are barking their fool heads off!"

"Aye," the constable agreed. He sounded weary. "Perhaps there's a fox out. Or a rabbit."

"What about the tor?" someone else asked. "There's a big tor up here. Lynch Tor. Now where did *that* go to?"

I sat up at that question. From the sounds of their voices, they couldn't have been more than twenty yards away. How could anyone miss something as big as the tor? All they had to do was stretch out their hands and walk forward.

"I don't care where the tor is," the constable said. "I've seen enough tors for one night. The girl couldn't have gotten this far in this fog."

The dogs were still barking. *They* knew exactly where I was. But the constable was worn out. "Let's go home," he said. "We'll send out another party in the morning."

I held my breath as they left. Then I crawled out of the cave. I stepped out onto the granite ledge.

Nothing had changed. The dense white fog still blanketed the night sky. A fine mist fell around me. I saw the torches of the search party moving away. I heard the sounds of ponies whinnying. Below me I could see sheep moving, ghostly white. Except for the animals, I was alone. I was safe until morning.

I turned to go back into the cave. And then on the ledge, just behind me, I heard the sound of pipes playing.

Chapter 9

The Stranger on the Tor

I turned and saw a man standing directly behind me on the ledge. He wore a dark, hooded cloak. He held a pipe made of reeds in one hand. I think he had a beard. It was hard to tell. The hood hid his face. But I saw his eyes glittering, like an animal's. I knew that he was not from the village. I'd never seen him before. In fact, I'd wager that very few people had.

"W-who are you?" I stammered.

"How did you get up here? I-I didn't hear anyone climb up."

He didn't answer me.

He's one of the ghosts of the moor, I thought. The widow said they'd come after me. I realized that I could no longer hear the sheep or the ponies. The wind had stopped moving through the grasses. The moor was silent. It felt as if the whole world had suddenly gone still.

The silence terrified me more than anything that had passed that day. For I suddenly understood that there *was* real magic on the moor. There were powers in the stones and earth and sky that were not human. And I was facing one.

To my surprise, the stranger spoke. "You're a small thing to be causing so much fuss," he said. "Hardly worth hunting down."

I had no answer for that.

"You don't have to speak," he said.

I wondered if he could read my mind.

"This land belongs to me," he went on. "You may stay here safely this night. But only this night. Do you understand?"

I nodded. My knees were shaking. My lower jaw trembled. Nothing had ever frightened me so deeply. I couldn't even say what it was about him that scared me.

"Do you know why you may stay this night?" he asked.

I shook my head.

"I'll give you a hint," he said. "Lynch Tor was not always called by that name.

Its true name is Great Lynx Tor. Tonight you sleep in the shadow of the lynx. Do you understand?"

I didn't, but I nodded anyway. I was not about to question him.

"And I will give you a bit of advice," he added. "Heed me well, child."

I listened closely. I hoped he'd tell me how to lose the search party. Or at the very least, where to hide.

What he said was: "Keep to small places."

"Is that all?" I asked. Instantly, I knew I'd made a mistake. "I-I'm sorry, sir," I said quickly. "I didn't mean to be disrespectful."

"*That* is most fortunate," he said in a dry tone. He pointed to the cave. "Get some rest now. Morning will be here soon enough."

I started to the cave and stopped.

There was one thing I had to ask. "You said this land is yours," I began. "So you must know. Does the River Dart have a river god? And if it does, was it the river god that killed Gordon Potter?"

The hooded man acted as if he hadn't heard me

So I asked the real question. "Was it the cats I draw? Did they hurt Gordon? Did they call up something evil?"

For just a moment his eyes met mine.

"They're your cats," he answered. "You should know. Now get some sleep."

When I fell asleep for the second time that night, it was to the sound of pipes playing.

"Wake up, lazy bones!"

I opened one eye. Jeremy was

kneeling beside me. Light filtered in through the opening of the cave. I felt tired and a little dizzy. And I couldn't stop thinking about the man with the pipes.

"Hurry now," Jeremy said. "I've got food and flints. We'll have a quick breakfast. The latest news in Braunton is that they're starting another search for you this morning. So we have to get moving."

"Where?" I asked fuzzily. I was still half-asleep.

Jeremy waited until I sat up and opened my eyes. Then he said, "Did you ever hear of Crookwell?"

"No," I said. "What is it?"

"You mean, what *was* it?"

"All right," I said patiently. "What *was* it?"

"A village," he replied.

"And what is it now?" I asked. "A sparrow?"

"You're cranky this morning," he observed. "That's a good sign."

"Last night was very strange," I said.

The morning air was cold. I wrapped my arms around myself. I couldn't tell if I was shivering from cold or from fear.

"Crookwell was a tiny little village on this end of the moor," Jeremy explained. "About a hundred years ago it was abandoned. No one's lived there since."

"Why was it abandoned?" I asked.

"The usual nonsense. People saw ghosts and spirits. They were sure the place was haunted."

I thought of the man on the ledge last night. The man who was clearly more than a man. Of course, I'd never convince Jeremy of that.

"They fled the village?" I said as he handed me a scone.

"Everyone left within a month," he answered.

I bit down on the scone. "I suppose you think they weren't being scientific."

Jeremy put a hand on my arm. "This isn't a joke. There's a reason I'm telling you about this."

"Which is?"

"Crookwell is where you're going to hide!"

I began choking on the scone. Jeremy pounded my back and gave me some water.

"You can't be serious!" I said. "After all that's happened in Braunton—the disappearing crops. The animals torn to pieces. Gordon's death. And you want me to stay in a haunted village?"

"Please, Elizabeth," Jeremy said. "I

talked to my brothers last night. Widow Stevens has half the town convinced. They want to blame someone. You seem to be the easiest one. Mrs. Potter is even talking about hanging you for murder!"

I put my head down on my knees. "I don't want to talk about this," I said.

"We have to," Jeremy replied. "Don't you see? You have to hide where no one will search for you. Crookwell *is* perfect! They're all so superstitious, they wouldn't dare set foot there!"

"What if the town *is* haunted?" I asked. "What if your father is wrong? What if there are some things that science *can't* explain? What if ghosts or goblins really do exist?"

Jeremy was angry. "Do you want to go back to Braunton?" he demanded. "Gretchen is waiting. Just say the word, and I'll take you back. We'll be home in time for supper. But I don't know if you'll ever get the chance to eat it."

I sat in the cave and thought. It was an impossible decision. Which was worse? Going home to Braunton, where half the town wanted to hang me? Where even my own father could not face me? Or hiding out in a haunted village?

Chapter 10

The Haunted Village

"So this is Crookwell," Jeremy said.

We stood in the village common. A common is open land that belongs to the town. Everyone can graze their animals there. Usually, a common is green. Since no one lived in Crookwell, I thought it would be overgrown. I expected tall grasses and weeds.

Crookwell's common was bare brown earth.

"This is spooky," I said. "My father's fields look just like this. Something came through and ate everything. And it wasn't long ago, either."

"Elizabeth, this place has been deserted for a hundred years," Jeremy reminded me.

"That's plenty of time for weeds to grow," I said. 'I don't know if Crookwell is haunted or not. But whatever attacked our farms has been here, too."

Jeremy was silent. Then he said, "What do you want to do?"

A cold rain began to fall. "Let's go down into the town," I said.

We followed a footpath from the common. The first building we saw was the church. Its stone arches gleamed in the afternoon light. But the stained-glass windows were smashed. Only bits of colored glass remained.

Some of the houses in the town still stood. Most were ruins. A stone wall here, a front stoop there. The bare timbers of a barn on a hill. Three houses looked as if they'd burned to the ground. The village was silent except for the sound of Gretchen's hoofbeats.

Jeremy and I went into a cottage that had no door. It was perfectly empty. The floor had a giant hole in the center. It looked as if something had chewed through it. A dust ball drifted across the floor.

We both jumped at the sound of Gretchen whinnying. She sounded scared. We went back outside to calm her.

"What is it, girl?" Jeremy asked.

"Nothing," I answered as I stroked her neck. "She's nervous because there's nothing here. What's scary about Crookwell is that *we're* the only things alive. Everything that lived here is dead now."

"Maybe we should find another place to hide you," Jeremy said. His voice rose as the wind grew louder. I knew Jeremy had to start back. We could both feel a storm coming in.

I didn't want to be alone in this ghost town. A storm would make it even worse. But I had no other place to hide.

"I have to stay," I said. "You were right. This is the one place they won't look for me."

"Well, it won't be for long," Jeremy promised. "My dad will be back from Mrs. Finley's soon. Then he'll talk to the constable. He'll convince him that the widow is wrong."

Dr. Shaw had helped just about everyone on the moor. So most people listened to him.

"I'll bring you home as soon as it's safe," Jeremy promised. "And I'll check on you. I'll make sure you have food and water."

"What will the villagers say when you keep riding poor Gretchen across the moor?"

"The usual," Jeremy answered with a shrug of his shoulders. "Jeremy Shaw will never amount to anything." He looked down the street full of deserted houses. "Where will you stay?"

I didn't want to go back into the cottage with the broken floor. At the top of the street was a large white house. A sign on it said MERCHANT'S HOUSE. Like most of the other houses, it had no door. Boards were nailed over its windows.

"I'll stay in the grandest house in town," I tried to joke. But neither of us could manage a smile.

"Just be careful," Jeremy warned.

"I will be," I said as I watched him ride off.

Then Jeremy was gone. And I was alone in Crookwell. The sky went from pearl gray to charcoal. And rain began to hammer down.

I ran to the house at the top of the street. I stepped through the open doorway. Merchant's House had once been very grand. The rooms had high ceilings and tall windows. A huge hearth covered one wall. Oh, how I wished I had wood to light a fire!

Everything in the Merchant's House was covered with a thick coat of dust. Once the walls had been white. Now they were streaked with soot. Cobwebs hung from the ceilings. The wood floors were stained and split. The walls smelled of mildew. Spiders scuttled across the floor.

All the furniture was gone. But I could see marks on the floor where a table had once stood. A long staircase led to the second floor. I peered into the empty rooms. Bedrooms, dressing rooms, a bath, and a narrow linen closet lined with cedar shelves.

I wondered about the people who once lived here. Did the merchant's family have fancy dinner parties? I imagined the women in fine silk dresses. I could picture lamps with crystal prisms, mirrors framed in gold, and thick feather comforters and wool blankets in the linen closet.

It was in the Merchant's House that I began to wonder if places have memories. I wondered if the house remembered the merchant who built it. Or the children who slept there.

But as I walked through the house, I remembered that no one lived here No one ever would again. It was mine for as long as I stayed. I could do what I wanted.

I set my bag down in the dining room. I took out my charcoal. All around me were huge blank walls. They were better than sketch books. I'd never drawn anything very large. I never had anything large to draw on. Now I stepped up to the wall next to the hearth. And I began to draw a cat as big as I was.

I had never had so much space to draw on. I'd never been in a place where I knew no one would stop me. There were no cows to milk. No chores to do. I was very much alone. And I created company of my own choosing.

I drew cats eating and sleeping. I drew a tabby crouched to pounce. I drew two fighting toms. I drew a kitten curled in a ball. I thought of what the stranger had told me about Lynch Tor. And so on the largest wall, I drew a lynx. Its teeth were bared. Its claws were out. And its eyes seemed to glitter.

The light was fading fast. Outside, the storm had gotten worse. Rain lashed the house. The wind howled. I looked out through the door. The skies were nearly black. With the windows boarded up, the inside of the house was dark. Soon I could barely see. In the kitchen, I found a candle stub. I lit it with the flint. I drew cats until the candle's wick was gone.

The house was dark. And I was cold

and hungry. I ate some of the biscuits and cheese that Jeremy had brought me. Then I went upstairs to find a place to sleep.

The second-floor rooms were all dark. I'll sleep in the master bedroom, I thought. I liked the idea of having a whole house to myself. Even if it was filthy and empty.

I started toward the master bedroom. Outside, thunder crashed above the house. And for a second the hall was bright with white light.

It's just lightning, I told myself. But I was shaking, as badly as when I'd been on the tor. Because in that split second of light I saw a ghost. It was a man dressed in a long, black coat. He stood beside an open coffin.

I knew the coffin was meant for me. The man pointed to it. Then he pointed to me and laughed.

Chapter 11

Night of Terror

I don't remember running down the dark hallway. Or trying doors until I found the linen closet.

I do remember screaming until my throat was raw. I remember being unable to move. I stood there, sobbing. I knew that when the lightning flashed again, the man in the long black coat would be there. And he would put me in the open coffin.

The wind howled like a wild animal. Rain beat against the roof. Thunder shook the house. Still, I couldn't move. Then I heard something else. The high, clear notes of a reed pipe sang through the storm. And I heard the voice of the man on the tor. "Keep to small places."

The next thing I remember is being inside the linen closet. I was sitting on the floor. My back was wedged against the door. My whole body shook.

The inside of the closet was pitch black. It was cramped, so narrow that my knees pressed against my chest. I couldn't see a thing. Something that felt like a spider crossed my hand. I couldn't even scream anymore.

A terrible crashing sound came from the first floor. Lightning lit the house again. For a second I could see the inside of the closet through a crack in the door. And I could see the man from Lynch Tor. He stood facing me. His arms were crossed over his chest. His eyes glittered beneath his hood. Then he, too, vanished with the lightning.

I crouched against the closet door, listening. It was all I could do. The sounds from downstairs were like nothing I'd ever heard. I still hear them in my nightmares. Things—I couldn't imagine what—crashed and slammed. The floor beneath me shook. Something shattered into bits. Something else roared in fury. I heard a voice so loud it drowned out the thunder. And yet I couldn't understand it. It spoke in a language that does not belong to our world.

The screams were the worst. Screams of pain. Screams of things caught in terror. Screams of the dying. Screaming that went on for hours.

I couldn't move. But my terror changed. I stopped shaking. Instead I felt so sick I wanted to die. Had the man with the coffin returned, I would have welcomed him. I remembered Widow Stevens talking about the Evil. I hadn't known what she meant then. But listening to those sounds, I knew. The Evil was in the house with me. There was no mistaking it.

All I could think was that Widow Stevens was right. *I* had brought the Evil to the moor. Farms were destroyed. A three-year-old boy was dead. The house I was in was being torn apart. *And it was all because I drew cats.*

Chapter 12

The Evil Revealed

At some point I fell asleep. When I woke I saw a crack of sunlight beneath the closet door. It was morning.

Now what? I asked myself. I wanted to run from Crookwell and never return. Oh, how I wished I could vanish in the countryside. Or stow away aboard a ship and go to sea. But I knew that I had to return to Braunton. The cats I drew were evil. They'd taken enough lives. It was time to turn myself in.

I took a deep breath and opened the closet door. Step by step, I walked through the hallway. I dreaded going downstairs. I didn't know what I would find.

The first thing I saw was that the stairway was nearly gone. The banisters were smashed. Some of the stairs had been ripped out.

Slowly, I made my way down. I had to climb, almost as if I was climbing down boulders. Once again, I was shaking.

What I found at the foot of the stairs made me ill. First I was dizzy. A moment later I threw up.

When I was done being sick, I forced myself to look. Bodies littered the floor of Merchant's House. But they weren't human bodies. They were giant gray rats. Each one was twice the size of a man! Each had fangs the size of my hand!

I stood, stunned. What could have killed these monsters? I knew there wasn't a living being for miles. It couldn't have been another animal. Not even a cow was as big as one of the rats.

And then I looked at the walls. The charcoal cats I'd drawn were still there, hunting, playing, sleeping. But they were different, too. Each cat's mouth was red with blood.

I don't know how long I stood there, staring at the cats. It was long enough to know that they were not evil. It was the rats who'd raided the fields. The rats had mauled Jeremy's sheep and the other farm animals. And the rats had killed little Gordon.

I could almost hear the man on the tor, when I'd asked if my drawings were evil. "They're your cats," he'd said. "You should know."

Now I did. The cats had protected me. And they had killed the rats that were destroying our land.

I was still staring at the walls when the men from our village arrived. Jeremy stepped through the open door first. Behind him were his father and my father and the constable. His brothers and mine trooped in behind them.

"What have we here?" asked Dr. Shaw.

"Goblin rats!" said the constable. He stroked his chin. "My grandfather used to tell me about them when I was a boy. He said they lived in nests below the tors. I never believed him."

"Elizabeth, are you all right?" my father cried. He swept me into his arms.

"I think we owe the girl an apology," the constable said. "And our thanks."

Dr. Shaw shook his head. "I wouldn't believe it if I wasn't seeing it with my own eyes."

He went up to one of the rats and touched its stiff leg. Then he touched his hand to one of the cats' mouths. Wet blood dripped down his finger.

The doctor's jaw dropped open. "There must be a scientific explanation," he murmured.

Jeremy just looked at me in my father's arms. Our eyes met and we almost laughed.

Chapter 13

Fifteen Years Later

It's been fifteen years now since the cats killed the goblin rats. I went back home with my father. Life returned to normal. The moor still had its ghosts and legends. But none of them did any real harm.

As for me, I was still useless at chores. I never learned to bake a proper pie. I still liked to waste my time doing you-know-what. But no one ever yelled at me again. They let me draw my cats. Mrs. Potter even said she was sorry for ever blaming me for Gordon's death.

Only the Widow Stevens stayed away from me, until last year, on the day I married Jeremy. She came up to me as we were leaving the church. She was still dressed in black, and still cranky.

"I'm sorry I caused you trouble all those years ago," she said.

"All's forgiven," I told her. "It's all in the past."

"I just want you to know you're not Evil," she said loudly.

"We do know," Jeremy said with a smile.

She squinted at me and added, "But you're still a strange lass."

She was right about that. I've learned that I'm not like everyone else. I see things that few other people see. I found out that the last man to own

Merchant's House was an undertaker. It was his ghost I'd seen that night.

Now and then, when I walk the moor I still see the man with the pipes. He's not Evil either. I like to think of him as a protector.

He and Great Lynx Tor protected me that night. You see, I believe that the moor has a certain spirit of its own. Sometimes when I'm standing on a windblown tor, I feel it watching me. It remembers all the people and animals who've lived there. The knights from the Middle Ages and villagers from the Bronze Age. We are all part of it.

The moor and my cats and Jeremy saved my life. Sometimes what you love is what saves you.

Jeremy would say these beliefs are not scientific. But he would not say they are untrue. It was Jeremy who asked me to set this story down. He says that the twentieth century is almost upon us, and it will open us all to the world of science. So he thinks it's important that people know that there is not *always* a scientific explanation.

Jeremy is a doctor now. I am his wife. But I am also an artist. Paintings of mine hang in London and Paris. Mostly, I paint landscapes—the trees and rocks and skies of Dartmoor. I think you would know my work if you saw it. Because somewhere in every painting there's a cat.

ELLEN STEIBER lives in Tucson, Arizona, with two friends and three cats. She has always loved cats and ghost stories.

The idea for *Fangs of Evil* came from a Japanese folktale, "The Boy Who Drew Cats." The story was written down in English by Lafcadio Hearn. Hearn was born in 1850 and traveled all over the world. He lived in Japan from 1890 to 1904. He especially loved its ghost stories.

While this book is fictional, Dartmoor, in England, is a real place. It still looks much the way it did in the 1800s.

Big Bird
Follows the Signs

Featuring Jim Henson's Sesame Street Muppets

by Emily Perl Kingsley

pictures by
A. Delaney

KEEP
OFF
THE GRASS!

A SESAME STREET BOOK / GOLDEN PRESS BOOK
Published by Western Publishing Company, Inc.
in conjunction with Children's Television Workshop

"Hi, Betty Lou," said Big Bird. "Can you tell me how to get to the school? Prairie Dawn is playing in the school orchestra and I have to take her cello to her."

"Go down that way, Big Bird," Betty Lou answered. "Then just follow the signs. But you'd better hurry. It's almost time for the concert."

Big Bird stopped at
the corner.

"Oh, look! There's a
sign that says DON'T WALK.
Betty Lou said to follow the signs,
so I'd better not walk."

"Oh, boy. The sign says WALK. Now I can walk."

"There's another sign. It says DOWN.
I guess that means I should go down
into the subway," said Big Bird.

"Look at all the signs in here—
THIS WAY IN and PUSH. I'd better
hurry up and follow the signs."

"Oh, there's another sign. It says
BRUSH WITH FOAM-O!"
Big Bird sat down.

"It's a good thing I packed my
toothbrush in Prairie Dawn's cello case!"

"Wow! That sign says TO THE STREET."

Big Bird jumped up and ran out of the subway.

"What a silly sign! It says ONE WAY,"
said Big Bird. "Anybody knows I can only
walk one way!"

"This sign says STOP, so I'm stopping.
But, gee, I wonder how long I have to stop here."

"Oh, this sign says GO TEAM GO!
Now I can go!" said Big Bird.

"Here's another sign. It says NO LEFT TURN!
I guess that means I should go straight."

"Here's the school! But that sign says
SLOW—SCHOOL ZONE. I'd better slow down."

"Hurry up, Big Bird," called Prairie Dawn.
"The concert's about to begin."

"There are so many signs in here," said Big Bird. He yawned. "I wonder if there's one that says SLEEP. Boy, am I tired!"